# BOO! HISS!

## CYNDI MARKO

**ALADDIN**

New York   London   Toronto   Sydney   New Delhi

ALADDIN
Simon & Schuster Children's Publishing Division
1230 Avenue of the Americas, New York, New York 10020
First Aladdin hardcover edition August 2022
Text copyright © 2022 by Cyndi Marko
Cover illustration copyright © 2022 by Cyndi Marko
Interior illustrations copyright © 2022 by Cyndi Marko
All rights reserved, including the right of reproduction in whole or in part in any form.
ALADDIN and related logo are registered trademarks of Simon & Schuster, Inc.
For information about special discounts for bulk purchases, please contact Simon & Schuster Special Sales
at 1-866-506-1949 or business@simonandschuster.com.
The Simon & Schuster Speakers Bureau can bring authors to your live event. For more information or to
book an event contact the Simon & Schuster Speakers Bureau at 1-866-248-3049 or visit our website at
www.simonspeakers.com.
Designed by Heather Palisi
The illustrations for this book were rendered digitally.
The text of this book was set in Goldplay and Family Cat.
Manufactured in China 0522 SCP
2  4  6  8  10  9  7  5  3  1
Library of Congress Control Number 2021945988
ISBN 978-1-5344-2545-3 (hc)
ISBN 978-1-5344-8483-2 (pbk)
ISBN 978-1-5344-2546-0 (ebook)

For Troy.
Thank you for being my person.
Forever and always, no backsies.
xo

And big squishy thank-yous to
my editor, Karen, and my designer, Heather.

# CHAPTER 1

At the top of a dead-end street looms an old empty house.

Empty except for a ghost, that is.
Her name is Phyllis.

The ghost has a roommate.

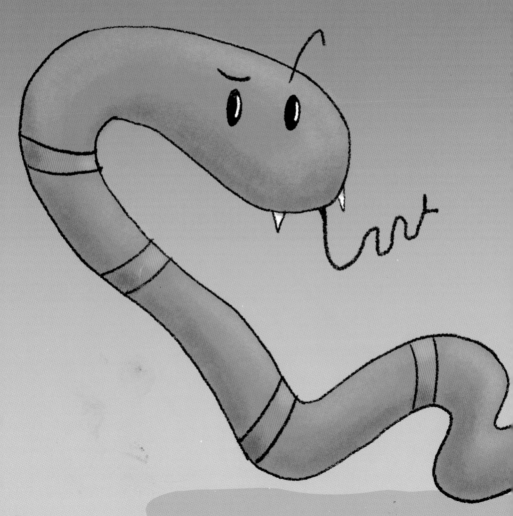

He's a snake. His name is Sheldon.

Mostly, the ghost and the snake get along like peas and (invisible) carrots.

11

Though sometimes they might get
a *little* snippy with each other...

# they always make up.

And that is how the ghost and the snake spend their time, day after day, year after year.

To the horror of the ghost and the snake,
humans of various sizes invade the house.

Medium Human, "Charlie"

C'mon, Doggo! Let's play ball!

Often has nose in a book

Bark!

Has a noisy hairy companion named "Doggo"

Kicks round things all over house

Tiny Human, "Bebe"

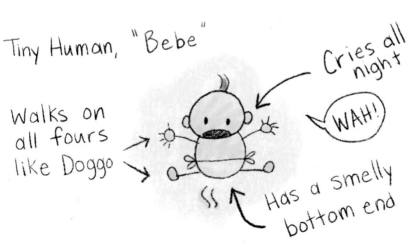

Cries all night

WAH!

Walks on all fours like Doggo

Has a smelly bottom end

The people touch the ghost's
and the snake's favorite stuff...

Ew. Throw out that moldy old chair.

But that's **MY** chair.

Out with the old...

But that's our stuff.

And the people make a *lot* of noise...

But the more the ghost thinks about it,

the more it isn't okay.

It isn't okay
*one little bit.*

The ghost and the snake try to come up with some good scares.

I could jump out of Charlie's underpants drawer.

I could hide in the flour container...

or the flower container!

Some of their ideas are more silly than scary...

I could pop up out of the toilet like a jack-in-the-box!

I could pretend to be the Ghost of Christmas Past!

In the end, they decide to go with good old-fashioned booing and hissing.

It's
SCARE
TIME.

Pack
your bags,
PEOPLE.

# CHAPTER 3

First the ghost and the snake
sneak up on the baby.

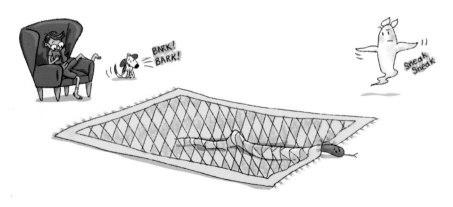

# But the baby isn't exactly scared.

In fact...

the baby thinks the ghost and the
snake are fun to play with.

*Super* fun to play with.

Phyllis and Sheldon beat a hasty retreat.

# CHAPTER 4

The next day, in the safety of the attic, the ghost and the snake come up with a new plan.

47

Sheldon and Phyllis
try to scare the boy...

who doesn't seem
to notice.

The ghost and snake give it
one last try...

# CHAPTER 5

Once again Phyllis and Sheldon return to the attic.

So they decide to SPY on the people and find out what really scares them!

With their new discoveries, Phyllis and Sheldon hatch their best, most scary plans yet.

The ghost and the snake sneak up on Dad...

The ghost and the snake are almost ready to give up.

# CHAPTER 6

And that's when the bickering starts.

You heard me.

## YOU'RE NOT SCARY!

What do you mean I'm not scary? I didn't see

## YOU!

scare the pants off anyone!

And then the ghost and the snake bicker over who is the MOST not scary.

The people hear lots of loud and strange...

# and scary...

and hair-raising noises.

And that's when the people decide to move out.

# CHAPTER 7

The ghost and the snake
can't quite believe it.

But the more they thought about it...

So the ghost and the snake come up with a NEW kind of plan.

And little by little, bit by bit, the ghost and the snake,

and the baby and the boy,

the mom,

the dad,

and the dog...

become a family—
boos, hisses, and all.

# CYNDI MARKO

writes and draws books for kids, but she doesn't mind if adults read them too. Cyndi is the author and illustrator of the Kung Pow Chicken early chapter book series, *This Little Piggy: An Owner's Manual* and *Boo! Hiss!* graphic novel chapter books, *Gilly's Monster Trap* picture book, and the Sloth Sleuth middle grade graphic novel series. She currently lives in British Columbia, Canada, with her two noisy, freeloading roommates, Cathulhu and Salem P. Cat.